Coal Mine
Peaches

by Michelle Dionetti
illustrated by Anita Riggio

ORCHARD BOOKS ❧ NEW YORK

ORCHARD BOOKS
A division of Franklin Watts, Inc.
387 Park Avenue South
New York, NY 10016

Manufactured in the United States of America
Printed by General Offset Company, Inc.
Bound by Horowitz/Rae

Book design by Alice Lee Groton

10 9 8 7 6 5 4 3 2 1

The text of this book is set in 16 point Berkeley Old Style Medium.
The illustrations are watercolor reproduced in full color.

LIBRARY OF CONGRESS CATALOGING-IN-PUBLICATION DATA
Dionetti, Michelle, date.
Coal mine peaches / by Michelle Dionetti ; illustrated by Anita Riggio.
p. cm.
Summary: Beginning with her grandfather's boyhood in Italy, a young girl
describes his arrival in the United States and the life he lived with her
grandmother and their children and grandchildren.
ISBN 0-531-05948-0.—ISBN 0-531-08548-1 (lib. bdg.)
[1. Grandfathers—Fiction. 2. Italian Americans—Fiction.
3. Family life—Fiction.] I. Riggio, Anita, ill. II. Title.
PZ7.D6214Co 1991 [E]—dc20 90-28693

To the memory of
my grandfather, Peter Ferretti,
my grandmother, Victoria Dondero Ferretti,
and my cousin, Andy Petrini,
who took me into the mines,
and gave me coal mine peaches.   —M. D.

For my father,
Frank D. Riggio,
and the memory of my mother,
Clotilda Taranto Riggio.   —A. R.

When my grandfather was a little boy,
he lived in a coal-mining town.

He and his brothers worked underground in the breakers of
the mine, picking slate out of coal.

To keep his brothers happy when the cold made their hands
red, my grandfather told them stories.

"You wait until summer!" he began. "It gets so hot in
the heart of the mine that peaches grow out of the coal!"

"Oh, Peter!" They laughed. "What a story!"

But in the summertime, when they ate small purple plums the
size of coal nuggets, my grandfather said,

"What did I tell you? Coal mine peaches!"

And they believed him.

When my grandfather became a young man,
he went to the city of New York to seek his fortune.
He lived in a boardinghouse there with other young men
who'd come to seek their fortunes.

Together they built the Brooklyn Bridge.

At night they sat at Mrs. Riposa's long, crowded table
for their supper of pasta, potatoes, and bread
and told one another stories.

"We're rich men!" cried my grandfather.
"We're building the Brooklyn Bridge!
   We get a penny to keep,
   a penny to spend,
   and a penny to send home to Ma!"

Nearby in the crowded city
lived a young woman with quiet eyes
and black hair so long she could sit on it.
My grandfather thought she was beautiful.
He asked her father to introduce them.
Her father saw that Peter was a fine
hard-working Italian man, so he agreed.

The young woman's name was Victoria.
She worked in a chocolate factory by day
and her father's restaurant by night.
She was gentle and shy.
My grandfather brought her flowers.

Together they took long walks.
On Sundays they took the ferry to Staten Island.

My grandfather told Victoria stories about his family.
Victoria told my grandfather about Genoa, Italy,
where she was born.

Victoria was very shy,
but she was not shy with my grandfather.
He made her laugh.

Victoria married my grandfather,
and so she became my grandmother.

They had five children, three boys and two girls.

They had a garden where they grew eggplant
and tomatoes, green pepper and basil.
They had a coop full of chickens,
so they had plenty of eggs, and meat on Sundays.
They had a small vineyard, so they had grapes and wine.
They had all of these things, but they were very poor.

My grandfather worked hard
cleaning buildings.

My grandmother worked hard
raising their children.

At night when my grandfather
came home for supper, he would
smell tomatoes simmering
on the big black stove
and fresh bread baking in the oven.

When they were all gathered
around the big wooden table,
my grandfather told them stories.

"Someday," he began,
"you will have children too.
When they come to visit,
I will tell them about

Andrew with chapped hands
from chopping wood,
Louise worried about
tomorrow's spelling lesson,
Domenic with the gum
he's not supposed to chew
stuck in his hair,
Angie with curls so long
they bounce like a yo-yo,
and Jimmy, with shoes so tight
they make his ears stick out!"

And so it was, when I was a little girl.
We went to visit my grandparents every Sunday.
After church we drove in our fat green car
to their narrow house high on a hill.

My grandmother wore slippery black dresses
with tiny flowers on them,
and a black sweater with rhinestone buttons
that I thought were diamonds.

My grandfather wore flannel shirts and baggy pants,
and he liked to tell me stories.

"Tell about when I was a little girl, Grandfather!"
I would beg.

And so my grandfather would begin:

"When you were a little girl,
you had a yell as big as a siren! Yes!
When you cried for your supper,
all the neighbors would come
with water to put out the fire!

"'No fire!'" I'd say. "'It's just my granddaughter—
the family opera singer!'"

I loved the things in my grandfather's house.
In the kitchen was a fat black stove
and a funny arched radio as tall as I was.
In the parlor hung a photograph
of my grandmother and grandfather
and their very first baby in a long white dress.

"Who's that baby, Grandfather?" I would ask.

"Let me look," said my grandfather.
"Yes, yes, that's right—the handsome one's me,
the thin one's your grandmother,
and that baby is Andrew, your father!"

"How can that baby be my father?"

"Just like you, Andrew grew up.
First he was a baby, then a boy, then a man.
When Andrew became a man, he fell in love
with a woman named Monique."

"That's my mother!" I cried.

My grandfather nodded.

"Andrew married Monique.
And they had you.
You are their only child."

I was my grandfather's oldest
grandchild. Other babies came—
two from Aunt Louise's family,
three from Aunt Angie's,
three from Uncle Jimmy's,
and seven from Uncle Dom's!

In the fall when the grapes were ripe,
all the uncles and aunts and cousins came to harvest them.

"Grandfather!" we begged when we all came to visit.
"Tell about when our parents were little!"

And so my grandfather would begin:

"When your parents were children, I put them to work—
Andrew in the woodpile,
Louise with a rake,
Angie and Jimmy in the garden,
and Domenic to clean out the chicken coop.

Andy, he chopped,
Louise, she raked,
Dom, he complained,
Angie, she sang,
and Jimmy, he ate all the green beans!"

At night, while the children were supposed to be asleep,
the grown-ups sang and told stories.
While they laughed, we crept to the top of the stairs
so we could listen too.

"We're rich men!" cried my grandfather.
"We're making the grapes into wine!
  A glass to my wife,
  a glass to long life!
  A glass to the grapes on the vine!"

In the wintertime when it was cold,
we sat in the kitchen to visit,
and listened to the big radio that was as tall as I was.
My grandfather shined all our shoes.
He had hands like a wool blanket, rough and warm.
I watched them fly as he polished.

"You must be rich, Grandfather!" I said, thinking
about how hard he worked.

"Rich, you say!" he replied. "If I had three pennies
at one time, I'd juggle them!"

I kept close watch, but I never saw him juggle.

While my grandfather shined shoes,
my grandmother rolled dough for pasta.
She cut it into wide ribbons for lasagna
or thin ones for spaghetti.
The black wood stove cooked our dinner and kept us all warm.

At Eastertime all the cousins came
to my grandmother and grandfather's house.
We wore our very best clothes.
At dinner we ate all the food we could hold,
and still there was food left over.

After dinner we searched for colored hard-boiled eggs
in the roots of the weeping willow tree.

"That Easter Bunny is no bunny!"
my grandfather teased while we searched.
"He's a rooster in disguise!"

"Oh, Grandfather!" We laughed. "What a story!"

In the summertime my mother and grandmother
sat on the lawn swing next to the weeping willow tree.
My father pushed the lawn mower across the grass.
My grandfather and I fed seeds to the chickens.
The fat hen Constanza always pecked my feet for more.

"That fat Constanza!" My grandfather chuckled.
"She peck-a, peck-a, peck-a!"

Sometimes, in the summertime,
my grandfather told me to hold out my hands,
and he filled them with small dark plums.

"When I was a little boy," he began,
"I lived in a coal-mining town.
It got so hot in the heart of the mine,
that peaches grew out of the coal!
And here's some for you,
some coal mine peaches!"

And I believed him.